The Big Storm

Story by Mike Kaye
Illustrations by Sarah Nelson

For
Liam and Simon

To order additional copies of this book, contact:
Xlibris
1-800-455-039
www.xlibris.com.au
Orders@Xlibris.com.au

The
Big Storm

Story by Mike Kaye
Illustrations by Sarah Nelson

Dump Truck Dave loves working on Barcoo mine, with his friends, Harry and Sammy, and Wendy the Water Cart. Miner Mike is in charge of the mine.
He oversees the 6 wheeled drive trucks, with the help of his trusty light vehicle, Tilly.

They might be smaller than the other trucks at the mine, but Dave, Harry, Sammy and Wendy are very strong.
They work hard building roads and dams, removing fallen trees and carting gravel.

Norm, the Heavy Haul truck, is much bigger
than Dave.
He carts the minerals up from the mine.
"We do all the hard work here," Norm brags.

"You 6 wheelers are too small to work on the mine!" Norm teases.
"Come back when you're bigger," he says, bumping and pushing the smaller trucks.
Norm's behaviour upsets Dave, Harry and Sammy.
His teasing hurts their feelings.

"Don't worry, Norm" says Dave. "We can save you."
"How?" asks Norm and Miner Mike, puzzled.

"We might be smaller than the other trucks at the mine, but we are strong," says Dave.
"We can carry gravel from the quarry, to repair the road and together we can pull all the heavy haul trucks out of the mine, to safety."

Miner Mike chains Harry to Wendy, and Dave to Sammy. Together they tow Norm and the other big trucks, up the steep hill, to safety.

"Phew! That was close," exclaims Norm.
"If it wasn't for you, we all would have drowned."

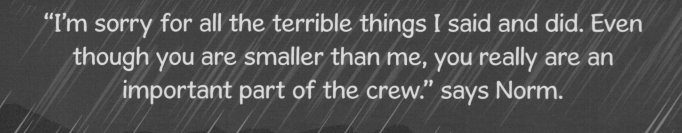

"I'm sorry for all the terrible things I said and did. Even though you are smaller than me, you really are an important part of the crew." says Norm.

"No worries" says Dave. We are all stronger, when we work together as a team".
"Yes," says Norm. "Big or small, we all have important jobs to do, at Barcoo Mine."

The Crew

Dave knows the answer to most problems. "No worries". He is the most experienced.

Sammy is young and rushes to jobs often without thinking first.

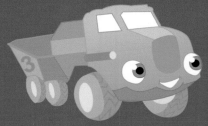

Harry is shy and follows all orders given to him.

Wendy loves being part of the team and always wants to be involved

Norm has learnt that bullying is not a good thing. Now he is a team player.

Gracie is a perfectionist. She takes her time to make her job neat and tidy.

Doug is tough, and bigger the rock to move or dam to build the better.

Larry is the quiet one and goes about his job without any fuss.

Danny loves the hard, dirty work of digging and loading.

Tilly is Mike the Miner's faithful light vehicle.

Mike is easy going and runs the mine fairly and with safety in mind at all times.

Printed in the United States
By Bookmasters